Contents

Meet Bird!

Bird is always around watching Bob and the rest of the team as they work. See if you can spot him on every page in the book!

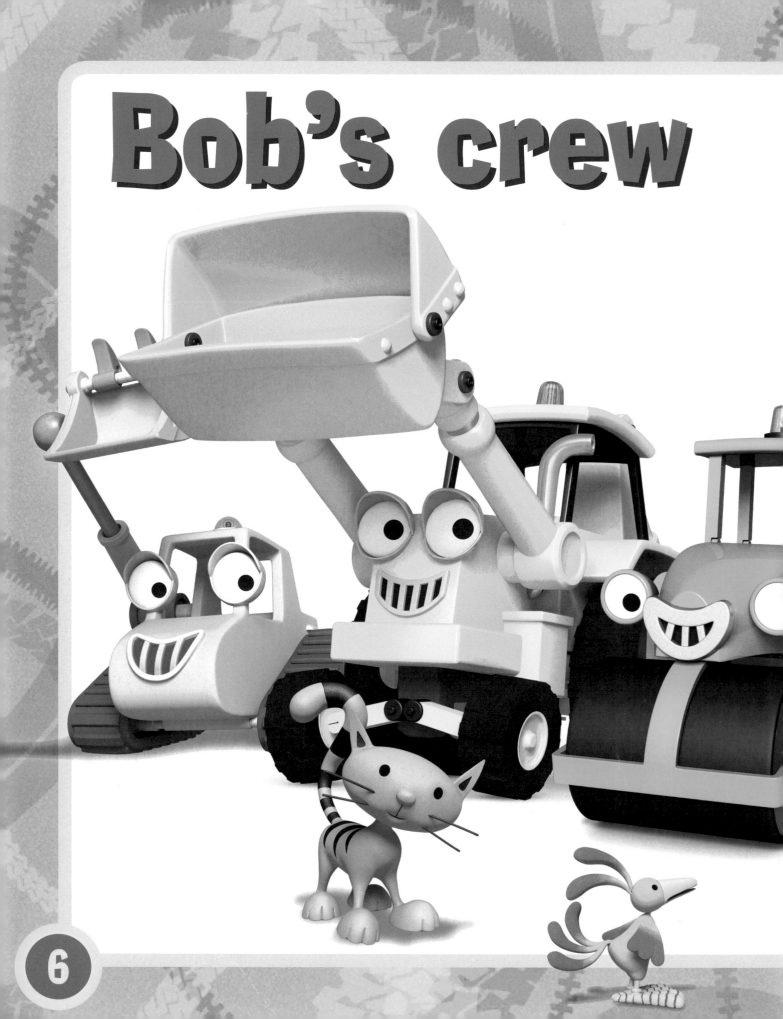

Bob's crew

Bob the Builder and his business partner Wendy have a hard-working team of special machines to help them build and fix things for the people of Fixham Harbour. Bob, Wendy and everyone in the team work together to get each job done, and they often learn new skills from each other along the way. In this book we'll take a look at the machine team and find out how they work and what they can do.

Scoop

Scoop is a special kind of digger called a backhoe loader. At the front he has a large bucket for scooping and loading earth, sand and gravel. At the back he has a mechanical arm with a small bucket for digging holes and trenches. Scoop loves a challenge and is happy to lead the rest of the crew on projects.

Tipping mechanism

Arm extended

Fact file

Hydraulic fluid is a special kind of liquid used in some types of moving machinery. It is pumped through pipes and into the cylinders in Scoop's arms. The hydraulic rams inside the cylinders are pushed by the fluid, making them extend Scoop's arms and move his buckets.

Large bucket for scooping

Small bucket for digging

Hydraulic ram

Powerful engine

Drive shaft

Front axle

9

Roley

Roley is a roadroller and his job is to pack down new roads and paths to make them hard and smooth. Instead of wheels, he has three large, smooth rollers, which even out lumpy surfaces when he drives over them. Like all roadrollers, Roley is very heavy, which means that he is much slower than the rest of the machine team.

Steering gear

Engine

Front roller

Flashing light

Fact file

Roadrollers like Roley are often called 'steamrollers' because they used to be powered by steam engines. Today most roadrollers have diesel engines, although some steamrollers were still being used as recently as the 1970s.

Chain drive to rear rollers

Rear roller

Lofty

Lofty is a large, strong mobile crane. He has six wheels to keep himself steady so that he can lift heavy loads up high. As well as his lifting hook, he also likes to use an electro-magnet, a grabber and a demolition ball. Unfortunately, Lofty is afraid of heights, mice and loud noises!

Telescopic crane boom

Gears to rotate crane boom

Very large and powerful engine

Six-wheel drive

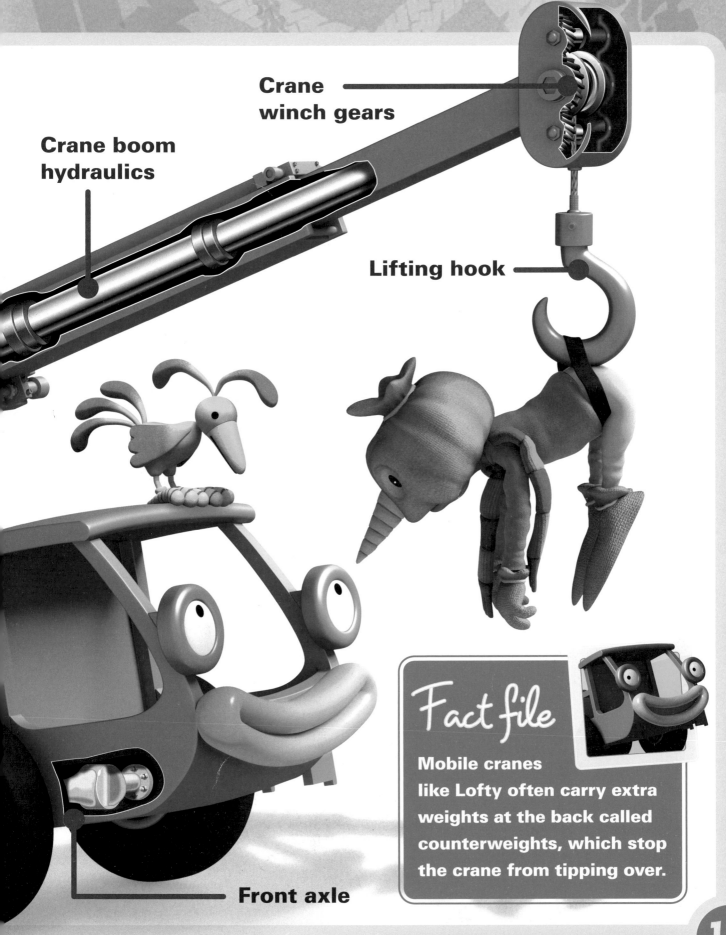

Crane winch gears

Crane boom hydraulics

Lifting hook

Front axle

Fact file

Mobile cranes like Lofty often carry extra weights at the back called counterweights, which stop the crane from tipping over.

13

Lofty's crane hook can be replaced by other attachments. These mean he can do different jobs and be an even more useful member of the team. Let's have a look at some of them here.

Wrecking ball

This solid metal wrecking ball is perfect for swinging into old buildings and knocking them down.

Magnet

An electro-magnet is a special magnet that can be turned on and off. It is used for picking up heavy scrap metal and loading it into trucks for recycling.

Lifting hook

This is Lofty's normal attachment. It is very strong and can lift big loads using ropes and chains.

Grabber

The grabber has three strong claws that can grasp objects like tree branches and rocks.

Drill

The drill attachment is used to drill wide holes deep down into the ground for telegraph poles, large posts and building foundations.

Muck

Muck loves to move and scoop up dirt and rubble with his large front bucket and dump it into his tipping load bed at the back. He is very big and powerful so he can carry heavy loads. Muck has caterpillar tracks rather than wheels so he can work in the muddiest parts of the site that the other machines can't reach.

Tipping load bed

Tipper hydraulics

Caterpillar tracks

Caterpillar tracks are used on cranes, diggers and other heavy off-road vehicles. The tracks are wide so that they spread the weight to stop the vehicle sinking into soft ground.

Powerful engine

Large bucket for bulldozing and loading

Drive chain

Dizzy

Dizzy is one of the most excitable and enthusiastic members of the machine team, and she is always ready to mix cement mortar whenever it is needed. She is small enough to move close to where the work is, and then move on as soon as the job is done.

Drive chain

Engine

Mixing drum

Wheel to tip drum

Fact file

Mortar is made up of four parts building sand and one part cement. These are mixed together with just enough water to make it sloppy enough to join bricks and blocks together to build walls.

Building a wall

It is important to overlap the bricks on different layers so that they hold together properly. Once the cement mortar has dried and turned hard, the wall is very strong.

Tumbler

Tumbler mixes cement on the way to the building site. The large drum at the back rotates and keeps the cement runny so that it can be poured to make foundations and floors for buildings. The drum tips and the cement pours out down the chute. The chute can be extended and moved around so that the cement is poured where it is needed.

Engine

Drum rotation gear

Drum

Mixing blade

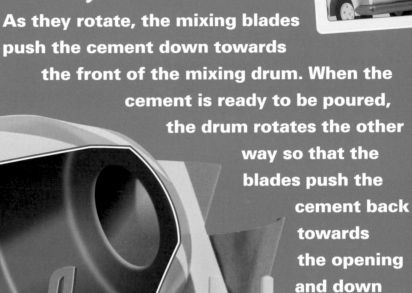

Fact file

As they rotate, the mixing blades push the cement down towards the front of the mixing drum. When the cement is ready to be poured, the drum rotates the other way so that the blades push the cement back towards the opening and down the chute.

Operator's ladder

Chute

Driveshaft to four rear wheels

Packer

Packer is a large semi-trailer truck, which means that he can unhitch one trailer and hitch another one. He has both an open and a covered trailer. Packer likes to make his deliveries on time and he has a powerful engine to help pull heavy loads but still go fast.

Open trailer

Double wheels

Brakes

Fuel tank

Exhaust stack

Wind deflector

Large engine

Steering box

23

Flex

Flex is a cherry picker, which is a special kind of crane for lifting people up high so that they can work. The crane lift, or 'boom', works by hydraulics, just like many of the other machines in the team. At the end of the boom there is a work platform so that Bob, Wendy, or anyone else can work safely on high jobs.

Engine

Radiator to cool engine

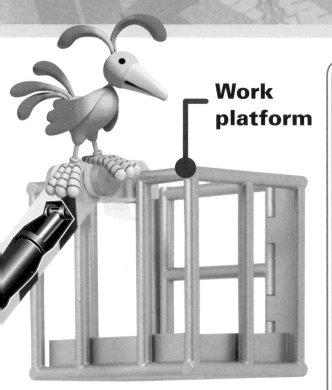

Work platform

Hydraulics

Boom

Rear axle

Fact file

Machines like Flex are called 'cherry pickers' because they were first made to help reach the high branches of fruit trees in orchards. Today they are used for all sorts of jobs, from fixing telephone lines to putting up Christmas lights.

Travis

Farmer Pickles and his tractor **Travis** are friends with Bob, Wendy and the machine team, and they try to help out whenever they can. Travis has a strong engine and gearbox so he can pull very heavy trailers at low speeds. Travis has four-wheel drive and large wheels so that he doesn't get stuck in the mud.

Fact file

Tractors are designed to do one thing very well and that's pull all sorts of trailers and different kinds of farm machinery. A 'power take-off' at the back means that the tractor engine can also power certain types of machinery such as hay balers and grass mowers.

Rear-wheel drive shaft

Steering column

Strong engine

Exhaust

Radiator fan

Gearbox

Front-wheel drive shaft

Scratch

Scratch is a digger, but he is very small and light. This means he can work in tight spaces where larger diggers, like Scoop, can't go. He also has caterpillar tracks to make sure he can always get around on muddy building sites. So, although he is small, Scratch is a very useful member of the machine team.

Fact file

Scratch has two claws on his front bucket so that he can grab things and pick them up, just like a crane. He can lift rocks, tree branches and even building materials such as bags of sand or cement and then carry them around the site to where they are needed. The claws also help to loosen hard ground when Scratch is digging.

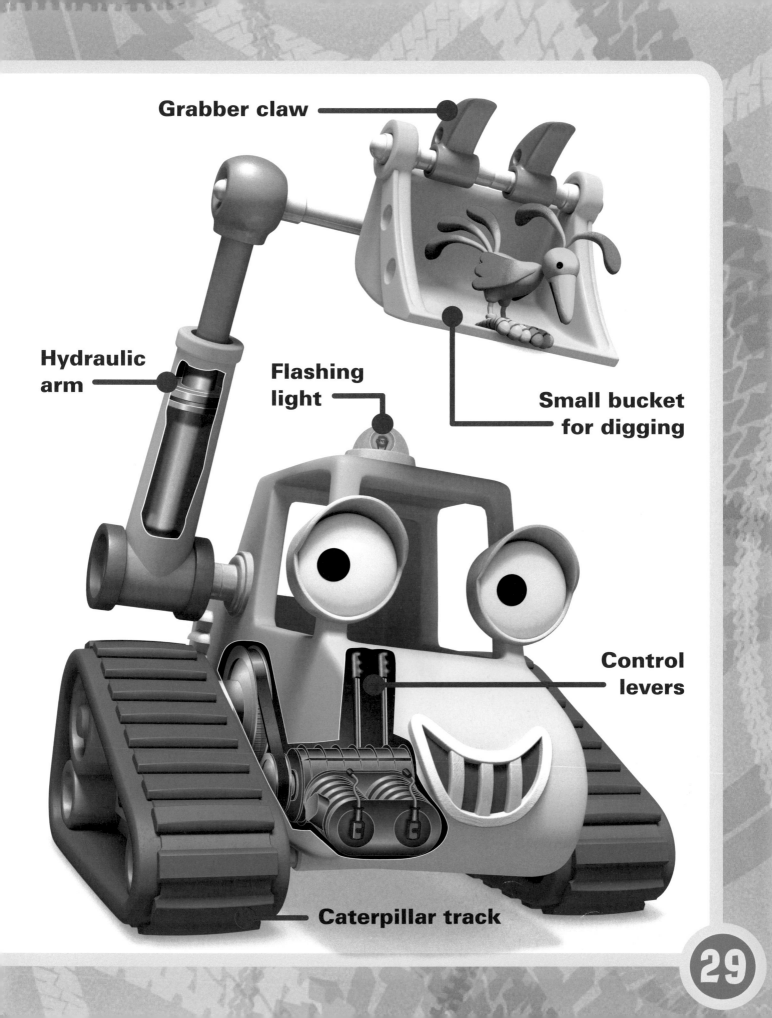

Grabber claw

Hydraulic arm

Flashing light

Small bucket for digging

Control levers

Caterpillar track

29

Rubble

Rubble is a large dumper truck and by far the biggest member of Bob's machine team. He can carry huge loads to and from wherever they are needed because he has a big, powerful engine and big wheels with wide tyres to stop him sinking in the mud. Even though he is huge, Rubble is very gentle and he often comes up with good ideas.

Fact file

Large dumper trucks like Rubble are specially made for working in places such as big construction sites, as well as mines and quarries. They have very large wheels (almost as tall as Bob!) and wide off-road tyres so that they can get close to the diggers and loaders where the work is being done.

Dumper tipping hydraulics

Rear axle

Large tipping trailer

Large, powerful engine

Front axle

Gripper

Gripper is a crane with caterpillar tracks, so he is ideal for working on muddy building sites where cranes with wheels can't go. Tracked vehicles are not very good for driving on the road and so Gripper needs to be transported on a lorry between jobs. Gripper is very strong and he has a second winch at the front, which makes him even more useful.

Fact file

Cranes like Gripper are called crawler cranes because of their caterpillar tracks. Other cranes need supports to stop them falling over, but crawler cranes are very steady because their tracks are heavy and help to spread the load. Crawler cranes can also carry heavy loads around the building site.

Track drive chain —

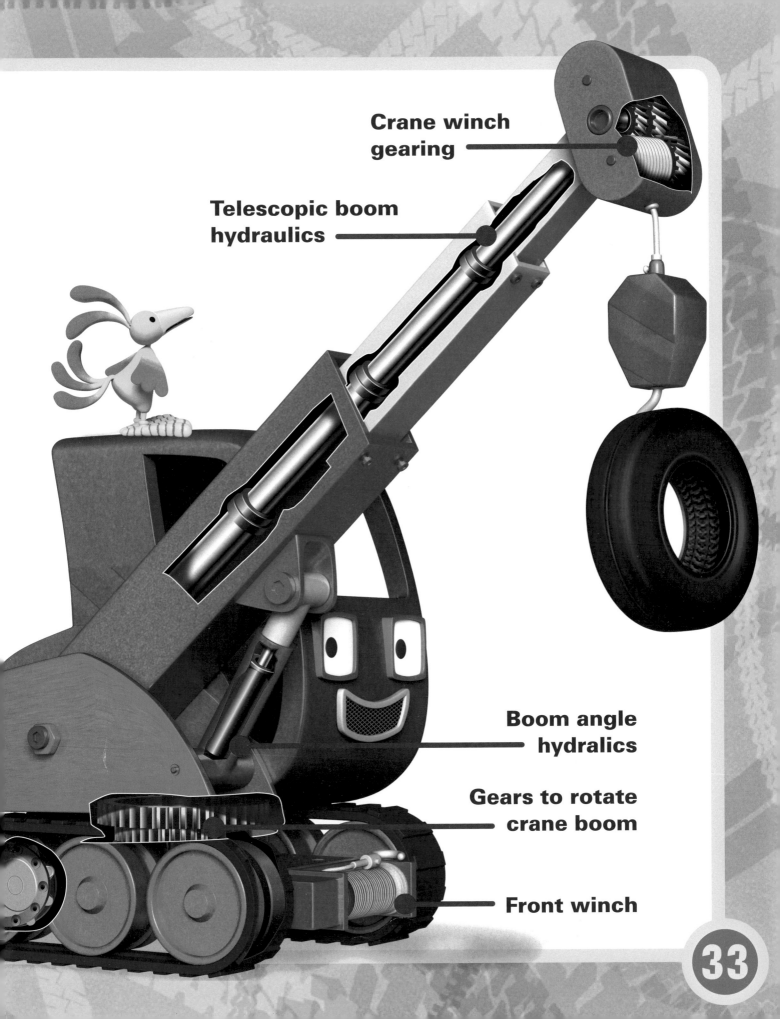

Crane winch gearing

Telescopic boom hydraulics

Boom angle hydralics

Gears to rotate crane boom

Front winch

33

Grabber

Grabber is a heavy tracked excavator with a special type of large bucket called a clam shell. He also has a bulldozer blade at the front so he can push great mounds of earth around, using his powerful engine and caterpillar tracks. Just like Gripper, Grabber cannot drive on the road and so he has to be transported on a lorry.

Fact file

Grabber's front bulldozer blade is ideal for 'grading', which means smoothing out rough ground. This makes a smooth flat surface, which is suitable for laying roads, paths and building foundations. Other bulldozer blades are more curved and have sides so that they can catch more earth and push it out of the way.

Clam shell bucket

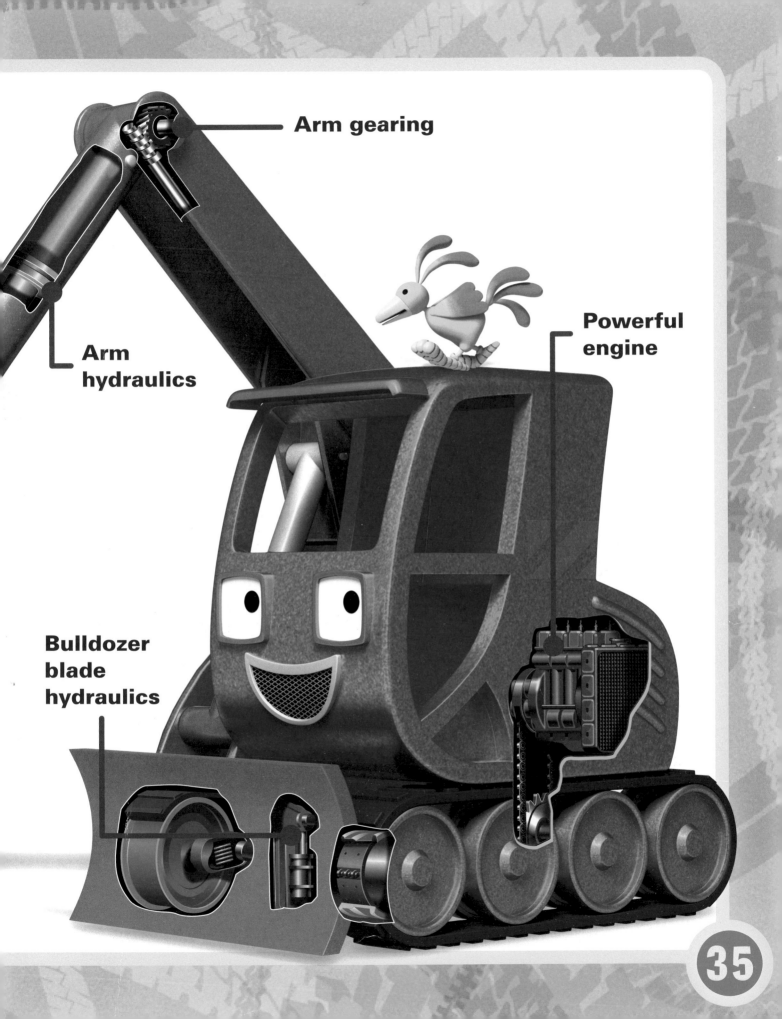

Arm gearing

Arm
hydraulics

Powerful
engine

Bulldozer
blade
hydraulics

Scrambler

Scrambler is an all-terrain vehicle (ATV), or quad bike. He is small and light with big knobbly tyres, so he is able to scramble over rough ground, and he is very fast. Scrambler can also pull small trailers, which means that Bob can take tools and materials to jobs in places that are hard to get to.

Fact file

Quad bikes come in all shapes and sizes. Some are small and have their engine in the middle like a motorbike. Others, like Scrambler, are larger which means that they can carry loads on their rack and pull trailers.

Rock guard

Carrying rack

Engine

Front brake

Suspension springs

Splasher

Splasher is a very special kind of vehicle because he is amphibious, which means that he can move on land and in the water, just like a boat. He has six-wheel drive so he can climb over rocks and slippery surfaces and 'balloon' tyres, which spread his weight so that he doesn't sink in soft mud, sand or swampy ground. This makes Splasher's six wheels almost as good as caterpillar tracks for driving off-road.

Fact file

When he goes in the water, Splasher uses two propellers at the back. They are powered by his engine. Instead of using his wheels to steer, he has rudders behind his propellers to help him turn in the water.